Thomas Baas

the Pied of Piper Hamelin

LITTLE
GESTALTEN

There once was a little town in the north of Germany called Hamelin. It was a prosperous and thriving town protected by stone walls. The townspeople of Hamelin led an easy life, but that alone didn't satisfy them. They spent their time indulging in lavish parties. While the adults enjoyed a carefree lifestyle of endless merriment, children were thought to cause nothing but trouble.

Then, one day, a terrible event occurred…
It was Christmas Eve in the year 1283; the people of
Hamelin were busy preparing to celebrate the holiday.
The scents of their feasts wafted throughout the town—
delectable aromas of ham, turkey, bread, tarts, and cakes.
In the midst of this excitement, nobody noticed that
a rat had snuck in through one of the town gates.

It was followed
by a second rat,
then a third …

After a few minutes, there were
a few hundred rats; after a few
hours, there were more than a
thousand. It was not long before
they invaded the entire town.

Nothing could stop these big black furry rats with beady eyes, pointy teeth, and scaly tails. They slid through doors, climbed up gutters, and crept into people's homes through their chimneys.

Once inside, the rats threw themselves onto the specially prepared Christmas food and began to eat it all. The townspeople tried to defend themselves and save a part of their dinners, but for each rat they killed, a hundred would appear.

By Christmas morning, there was almost nothing
left to eat. The rats were everywhere—inside
cupboards, between bed sheets, and in people's
pockets digesting their feasts.

On the third day, when there was absolutely no food left, the rats began devouring pillows, books, curtains, and even tables and chairs! They unleashed their voracious fury on animals bigger than them, sparing neither dogs nor cats. At night, they would sink their teeth into people's legs; no one was able to sleep.

Panicked, the townspeople gathered in front of Hamelin's town hall and begged the mayor to intervene. He ordered the most powerful poison from the apothecary and demanded that it be used in all of the mousetraps that could be found.

Alas, the rats were so clever and hearty that they avoided
all the traps laid out across the town and savored the
poison as if it were candy.
Desperate, the mayor announced that he would give a
thousand gold coins to whoever could free Hamelin
of this ordeal.

On the fourth day, a stranger came to Hamelin and
presented himself at the town hall:

"I heard you were offering a thousand gold coins to
whoever could rescue the town from these rats."

"That is true," replied the mayor, "But who are you?"

"I am known as the Pied Piper, and I know how to get
rid of these rats."

"Well, show us what you can do! If you succeed, I will give
you your reward."

The stranger calmly walked toward the main square. He took an ordinary small pipe made of black wood out of his satchel and started to play a strange melody. As soon as the first notes could be heard, the rats interrupted their relentless quest to eat everything in sight to listen to the piper's tune. Then, suddenly, they all leapt into the streets to gather around him. Soon, the main square was packed with thousands of entranced rats.

Still playing, the stranger began to walk toward the town gates. A gruesome yet tame procession followed his steps as the rats departed from Hamelin.

The Pied Piper reached a bridge above a nearby river and stopped there. The spellbound rats, however, kept going and threw themselves into the glacial waters.
It was over. All of Hamelin's rats were drowned.

Hamelin had a great reason to start celebrating again. The townspeople were singing, dancing, and laughing in the streets when the Pied Piper came to claim his reward.

"What do you want?" asked the mayor with disdain.

"I kept my promise," replied the stranger, "and now I come for my one thousand gold coins."

"One thousand gold coins for a little tune on a pipe? I will give you one hundred, not more. Take it or leave it!"

The Pied Piper looked the mayor straight in the eye and declared: "You will regret this."

He then left Hamelin without uttering another word.

Days went by and the townspeople had wholeheartedly returned to their lavish ways. The mayor congratulated himself on having tricked the stranger, and, indeed, everyone in Hamelin was happy about the way their encounter had gone.

But one morning, high-pitched notes resounded throughout
Hamelin. The townspeople immediately understood that the
Pied Piper had returned. This time, the melody was as joyful as
it was strange, a combination that drew all of the children of
Hamelin into the streets. They assembled around the stranger,
singing, dancing, and laughing.

Mesmerized by the piper's music, the children started following him without the least bit of fear. Their parents attempted to hold them back but failed. The group of children skipped across the bridge over the nearby river and disappeared into the mountains.
They were never to be seen again.

Some say that ever since that day, whenever the wind blows from the mountains, it brings along with it to Hamelin the echo of happy children laughing.

The Pied Piper of Hamelin

Illustrated by Thomas Baas
Original text adapted by Marine Tasso

Translated from the French by Noelia Hobeika

Published by Little Gestalten, Berlin 2016
ISBN: 978-3-89955-767-1

The german edition is available under ISBN 978-3-89955-766-4.

Typeface: Chaparral Pro by Adobe
Printed by Optimal Media GmbH, Röbel/Müritz
Made in Germany

The French original edition *Le joueur de flûte d'Hamelin* was published by
Actes Sud. © for the French original: Actes Sud, 2015. © for the English
edition: Little Gestalten, an imprint of Die Gestalten Verlag GmbH & Co.
KG, Berlin 2016.

For more information, please visit little.gestalten.com.

Bibliographic information published by the Deutsche Nationalbibliothek: The Deutsche Nationalbibliothek lists this publication in the
Deutsche Nationalbibliografie; detailed bibliographic data are available
online at http://dnb.d-nb.de.

This book was printed on paper certified according to the standards
of the FSC®.

FSC
www.fsc.org

MIX
Paper from
responsible sources
FSC® C108521